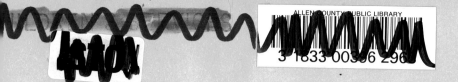

Ann Jonas

Greenwillow Books, New York

For Susan,
and of course,
Don, Nina + Amy

Printed in Hong Kong
by South China Printing Co.
First Edition   10 9 8 7 6 5 4 3 2 1

Library of Congress
Cataloging in Publication Data
Jonas, Ann.   The trek.
Summary: A child describes
her trip through a jungle and
across a desert—right
on the way to school.
1. Children's stories, American.
[1. Jungles—Fiction.
2. Deserts—Fiction.
3. Imagination—Fiction]   I. Title.
PZ7.J664Tr 1985   [E]   84-25962
ISBN 0-688-04799-8
ISBN 0-688-04800-5 (lib. bdg.)

My mother
doesn't walk me
to school anymore.

But she doesn't know
we live on the edge
of a jungle.

She doesn't even see
what's right outside our door!

There are creatures everywhere.
But they can't hide from me.

Some of my animals are dangerous
and it's only my amazing skill
that saves me day after day.

Look at that!
The waterhole is really
crowded today.

What will they do when this herd
goes down to drink?

Here's my helper, right on time.
Now we can cross
the desert together.

Those animals won't see us
if we stay behind the sand dunes.
Be very quiet.

That woman doesn't know
about the animals.
If she did, she'd be scared.

We missed the boat!
Now we'll have to swim
across the river.

Be careful! This jungle is full of animals.

The trading post at last!
No time to stop!

We're almost there, only the mountain to climb.

We made it!

SOME ANIMALS WE KNOW

MOOSE   ALLIGATOR   PORCUPINE   ALPACA   TURKEY   SPIDER

PANGOLIN   WARTHOG   ZEBRA   MONKEY   LIZARD   BONGO

CAMEL   PEACOCK   YAK   VULTURE   SEA LION   LEOPARD

MORE ANIMALS WE KNOW

OSTRICH   HIPPOPOTAMUS   KOALA   WATER BUFFALO   PIG   PYTHON

GORILLA   SWAN   RHINOCEROS   SHEEP   GIRAFFE   CASSOWARY

TURTLE   ELEPHANT   TIGER   ORANGUTAN   FISH   ORYX

FEB 02 1994

**DO NOT REMOVE
CARDS FROM POCKET**

DEMCO

GLORIA ESTEFAN

International Pop Star

Written by Shelly Nielsen

Published byAbdo & Daughters, 4940 Viking Drive Suite 622, Edina, Minnesota 55435.

Library bound edition distributed by Rockbottom Books, Pentagon Tower, P.O. Box 36036, Minneapolis, Minnesota 55435.

Printed in the United States.

Cover photo: Black Star
Interior photos: Black Star, Pages 5, 7, 11, 15, 24, 25
        Bettmann, pages 14, 18, 20, 28

Edited by Rosemary Wallner

Library of Congress Cataloging-in-Publication Data

Nielsen, Shelly, 1958-
    Gloria Estefan: International Pop Star / written by Shelly Nielsen.
        p.   cm. -- (Reaching for the Stars)
    Includes index.
    Summary: A biography of the Cuban-born pop star who sings, dances, composes, and records with the Miami Sound Machine.
    ISBN 1-56239-226-3
    1. Estefan, Gloria--Juvenile literature. 2. Singers--United States-- biography--Juvenile literature. [1. Estefan, Gloria. 2. Singers. 3. Rock music. 4. Cuban Americans--biography.]
    I. Title. II. Series.
    ML3930.E85N4   1993
    782.42164'092--dc20
    [B]   93-26000
                                                      CIP

                                                     MN   AC

TABLE OF CONTENTS

IN CONCERT

In the music arena, the waiting audience ripples with excitement. Suddenly mysterious dancers wearing sequined masks enter the stage. As the music builds, the dancers remove their masks one by one. Finally, just one dancer is still masked. She rips off the mask, letting a mane of dark, curly hair fall to her shoulders. The crowd roars. It's Gloria Estefan! She lifts the microphone and sings in her rich, strong voice: "Get on your feet, get up and take some action..."

Gloria Estefan can create so much excitement when she sings that her audience has to jump up and dance. Singing, dancing, writing, and arranging music...Gloria seems to do it all.

Gloria Estefan and the Miami Sound Machine in concert.

THE LONG ROAD

Born in Cuba in 1957, Gloria was still a baby when her parents brought her to America. Jose and Gloria Fajardo wanted to escape the government of Fidel Castro and create a good life for their beautiful, dark-haired daughter.

Gloria remembers those early years in Miami as "tough." She and other new Hispanic immigrants faced "a lot of prejudice." Perhaps it was her trademark upbeat attitude that helped get her through those hard times. Today she says she is grateful for the opportunities that America offered her.

Her start in music can be traced back to 1975. Gloria, now a teenager, wanted to start a band. Her parents knew a guy named Emilio Estefan who led a group called the Miami Latin Boys. He was from Cuba, too. Maybe he could give her some pointers. They invited him over.

After that first meeting, Emilio and Gloria didn't see each other again until they both attended the same wedding awhile later. The Miami Latin Boys were playing, and Emilio invited Gloria on stage to sing a few songs.

Hearing her voice again convinced him that Gloria must join the band.

Emilio and Gloria Estefan.

At first she refused. She couldn't be in a band and keep up with her school work. But Emilio promised she could sing just on weekends. Gloria loved music so much she couldn't say no. Soon she was singing lead with the group. The band changed its name to Miami Sound Machine.

For the next year, Gloria worked equally hard at her music and her studies. The band's popularity grew. She kept up her grades so well that she graduated as an honor student with a partial scholarship to the University of Miami. (She would later graduate from the University with a degree in psychology and communications.)

One day Emilio asked Gloria out on a real date. At first they both worried that dating would ruin their great working relationship. But they liked each other so much that the dates continued. Two years later, in 1978, Gloria and Emilio were married.

Today, if their schedules allow, they spend most of their time together—rehearsing, working through music, and traveling. Emilio quit performing in 1986 to devote himself to producing and managing Miami Sound Machine.

MOVING TO THE BEAT

Mix together Latin beats, urban pop, sweet ballads, rock, great dancing, and Gloria's unique voice. You'll get the hot sound of [Mia]mi Sound Machine.

[Millio]ns of fans around the world stand in ticket lines for hours, [fo]r a chance to hear and see Gloria in action. But she [remem]bers when the music business seemed closed to their style. "I'll never forget when we first did 'Conga.' This [produce]r told us that the song was 'too Latin for the Americans, [and] too American for the Latins.' I said, 'Thank you. That's exactly what we are! We're a mix.'" Getting that balance just right has taken years of work.

Rio, an album released in 1982, was recorded in Spanish. Gloria has always reached out to her Latin audiences. "We've never thought of abandoning Spanish for one moment," she says. "We will always record in Spanish. In fact, in the future I would like to release an album of ballads in Spanish. Hey, we're Latin Americans; Spanish is our Mother language....We're proud of our heritage."

Miami Sound Machine's first album in English was called *Primitive Love*. Released in 1986, it sold 1.5 million copies in the United States. All over America, fans rocked to the three top 10 singles: "Conga," "Bad Boy," and "Words Get In The Way."

The *Let It Loose* album released in 1987 went double platinum (sold 4 million copies) in America and spent two years on the charts in England. It had four top 10 singles—"Rhythm Is Gonna Get You," "Betcha Say That," "1-2-3," and "Anything For You."

The album *Cuts Both Ways* hit the No. 1 spot in England, going ten times platinum, and topped the charts in Scotland, Holland, Belgium, and Japan. In 1990, it went double platinum and spent five weeks at No. 1 on the adult contemporary chart.

Gloria Estefan considers her songwriting as the most important part of her work.

Along the way, Gloria has toured all over the world, created videos, and won many awards. Her hard work has paid off. Today Gloria Estefan and Miami Sound Machine are big in England and Holland. They are also picking up fans in other countries, including Scandinavia, Belgium, Spain, and Germany.

Gloria's success is due to her amazing combination of talents. She sings, dances, and composes. Songwriting is an important part of her work. When she sits down to write a song, she'll often work out the melody and lyrics on the guitar—her first love—or the keyboard. On *Cuts Both Ways*, she wrote seven of the album's 10 cuts.

What does she write about? Because of her family's experiences in Cuba, Gloria has strong political beliefs, but she prefers to keep politics out of her music. "Music to me is an escape," she says. "Love and emotions are things that everyone can share."

The formula works. Every album has outsold the one before it. And the fans around the world continue to dance through her concerts.

MEET GLORIA—SHE'S GREAT!

She's petite. She's positive. She's upbeat. She has a great sense of humor. Whether in a crowd or one-on-one, Gloria is easy-going and comfortable. In a business that depends on public appearances and interviews, that's important.

Radio disc jockeys like her because she is glad to give interviews. Whenever possible, she'll go out in person. If that's impossible, she'll give interviews by phone.

But she still likes a moment of privacy once in awhile. Emilio admits that, "When we go out we try to hide ourselves a little bit. We use different hats and glasses so that people won't recognize us, but most of the time people realize it's us."

THE GOOD LIFE

Gloria lives with Emilio and their son Nayib in a five-bedroom home on Biscayne Bay in Miami. The house is a little bit of Cuba right in Florida. The floors are covered with cool, white coral tiles. Rooms are lush with sculptures and exotic plants. Outside there's a hand-tiled pool. Jamaican and Cuban Royal palms rustle in the breezes off the bay.

Gloria Estefan is always positive and upbeat.

The Estefan's home on Biscayne Bay in Miami.

The Estefans enjoy spending time together on the poolside terrace. Gloria and Emilio say that at five o'clock each day they leave their business concerns behind and concentrate on each other. Family comes first.

Of her thirteen-year-old son, Gloria says, "He's more important to me than anything in the whole wide world." Because he is in school, the Estefans have worked out a unique way to include him in their hectic schedules. If a tour is scheduled during the school year, Nayib sometimes comes along—with a tutor. Or Emilio stays home with him, keeping in touch with Gloria by phone. But in the summers, the whole family can travel together.

About his son, Emilio says, "He's very inclined toward music. I think he's going to want to be a singer or...performer."

A DARK TIME

On March 20, 1990, Gloria, Emilio, Nayib, two Sound Machine staffers, and Nayib's tutor were traveling in their tour bus to a concert in New York. It was a beautiful sunny morning. Gloria stretched out on a couch in the forward cabin to take a nap. Around noon she woke when the bus stopped behind a stalled tractor-trailer. The sunny day had become dark and snowy. Suddenly, a semi-trailer truck behind them slammed into the back of the bus sending the bus crashing into the stalled tractor-trailer.

"The next thing I knew," says Gloria, "I was on the floor. I had a black eye and a strange, metallic taste in my mouth." Two chairs bolted to the floor near the couch were twisted sideways. Perhaps she had hit them when she flew off the couch. Gloria tried to lift her legs but could only move them a little way. Although the pain was horrible, she remembers thinking, "I'm not accepting this. I'm gonna get through this."

The impact had broken Nayib's collarbone and knocked Emilio right out of his shoes. The other passengers in the bus had only minor injuries.

Gloria Estefan, with her husband and son, met
President George Bush the day before the bus accident.

Rescue workers had to pull Gloria through the smashed-out front windshield. Then there was a 45-minute ambulance ride to the hospital where it was confirmed that her back was broken. A day later she was flown by air ambulance to another hospital for spinal surgery. Doctors implanted two eight-inch-long, quarter-inch-thick stainless steel rods in her spinal cord.

The operation left a 14-inch scar down the middle of her back. At first doctors said she would never dance again—and maybe never even walk. But Gloria was determined to get back on her feet. She went through months of intensive physical therapy, including weight training and aerobics. She wanted to get back her old strength, her old moves.

Flowers, cards, and letters came pouring in—a flood that started within hours of the accident. At one time Gloria estimated she had received 4,000 flower deliveries, 3,000 telegrams, and 30,000 postcards and letters. "Get well, Gloria!" they said. "We're rooting for you!"

"It definitely helped," Gloria says now. "So many people concentrating positively, praying for me. It was like an energy I could feel in the hospital. It helped me bear all that pain." Months later, in *Billboard* magazine, Gloria printed the following letter:

To My Friends-

Last March, after my bus accident, I discovered I had more friends than I ever dreamed possible. My recovery has required tremendous personal commitment, but it's been powered by the love and prayers and good wishes of so many people in this industry and so many fans around the world. For that support, my family and I will be forever grateful.

Gloria Estefan

On March 20, 1990, Gloria Estefan and her husband and son were in a terrible bus accident which left Gloria with a broken back. She is being wheeled out of the hospital after she underwent spinal surgery.

21

BACK INTO THE LIGHT

Gloria's injuries meant postponing Miami Sound Machine's world tour. To cheer her up during this difficult period, Emilio gave her two dalmatian puppies that were born on March 22, 1990, the day she had surgery. Ricky and Lucy—the Ricardos—helped her get through the hard times. Meanwhile, Gloria predicted that she would recover and come back better than ever.

A year later, she was on the road again—on a yearlong tour in Miami. "I'm still a little paranoid in traffic," she says, "and I'll probably be a little scared to take a nap the first few days. But I'll get over it."

She had already appeared on TV's American Music Awards (on January 28, 1991), and had released her comeback album, *Into the Light*. Things were definitely looking up.

One of the hardest challenges she faced was getting back to writing music. After all the time away from music, she had a bad case of writer's block. One day, months after the accident, Emilio convinced her to come to the studio.

He wanted her to hear a bit of a song he'd written the day Gloria was being carried by air ambulance to another hospital for surgery. He described how discouraged he had felt, thinking of all the pain ahead of Gloria. Then he had looked through the helicopter windows and had seen light breaking through the clouds.

When Gloria heard the song fragment, she sat down and began to write. "Everything just tumbled out," she says. "We finished that song right there. I tried singing for the first time that day too."

Today her comeback album, *Into the Light*, is selling wildly, fueled by her new hot videos and world tours.

She says that dance training since surgery has taught her "a whole new body language." She experiments with new moves; the metal rods in her back keep her from doing only the wildest ones. "I just have to make sure I don't do crazy things, like back flips off the stage," she says.

She has changed in other ways, too. "It's very hard to stress me out now," she explains. "It's hard to get me in an uproar because most things have little significance compared with what I almost lost....So many people got behind me and gave me a reason to want to come back fast and made me feel strong. Knowing how caring people can be, how much they gave me—that has changed me forever."

*Gloria Estefan helped victims of Hurricane Andrew
which ripped through the Miami area.*

The Estefans planned a benefit concert for the victims of Hurricane Andrew. Above, Gloria performs a song for the benefit.

Her chance to give back some of the caring came in September of 1992 when she and Emilio planned a benefit for the victims of Hurricane Andrew in Florida. The Estefans had survived the storm huddled in the control room of their South Miami recording studio—along with Gloria's mother, two friends, four dogs, and a bird. But when they came out, they saw the wreckage caused by the wind and rain and heard about all the people left homeless. The family went to work planning a benefit event. The money they raised would be donated to help Miami rebuild.

A sellout crowd of 55,000 came to see and hear Gloria and other stars. Nearly $2 million was raised. "I think we're ready for a little bit of fun," Gloria told the crowd. "Kind of shake off these blues."

Gloria also released a new song, "Always Tomorrow" and donated all the money she earned to help hurricane victims.

"You can't sit there and wallow," she said. "You weep for what's gone and then you move ahead."

DOWN-TO-EARTH, AT THE TOP

Interviewers say that success hasn't changed the Estefans. They're very down-to-earth. They still like to eat in their favorite Cuban restaurants. And they still love to go dancing. A sharp-eyed fan will occasionally catch them dancing to the music of a salsa band in a Miami Beach club.

"Hey," says Emilio, "just because we've made it doesn't mean I'm going to forget who I am and where I come from. Gloria and I still have the same friends that we had before the band became so popular. We will always be good to our friends. They've always been good to us."

Jorge Pinos, who is in charge of booking Gloria for tours around the world, says he enjoys working with the band. "They're a very together band. They don't do drugs, they don't drink....They're very hard workers."

Hard work has fueled Gloria's trip to the top—and hard work keeps pushing her ahead. She has risen to the top of the charts and has made an almost miraculous recovery from her injuries in a near-fatal accident.

Gloria Estefan's energy, ambition, determination, and matchless talent continue to make the music of Miami Sound Machine irresistible to fans around the world—and gets them on their feet, dancing.

Gloria Estefan touched her star on Hollywood's Walk of Fame.

GLORIA ESTEFAN'S ADDRESS

You can write to Gloria Estefan:

Gloria Estefan
8390 S.W. 4th Street
Miami, FL 33144

If you want to receive a reply, enclose a self-addressed, stamped envelope.

INDEX